Ada Lovelace
and Computer Algorithms

By Ellen Labrecque

21st Century Junior Library

Published in the United States of America by
Cherry Lake Publishing
Ann Arbor, Michigan
www.cherrylakepublishing.com

Content Adviser: Amelia Wenk Gotwals, Ph.D., Associate Professor of Science Education, Michigan State University
Reading Adviser: Marla Conn MS, Ed., Literacy specialist, Read-Ability, Inc.

Photo Credits: © Pixtural/Shutterstock Images, cover; © wavebreakmedia/Shutterstock Images, 4; © Pictorial Press Ltd/Alamy Stock Photo, 6; © Nicku/Shutterstock Images, 8; © Photos.com/Thinkstock, 10; © Science Museum London, Science and Society Picture Library/ Wikimedia (Mrjohncummings), 12; *Sketch of The Analytical Engine Invented by Charles Babbage* by Luigi Menabrea with notes by Ada Lovelace/ Wikimedia (Kaldari), 14; © Anna Bryukhanova/iStock, 16; © Tyler Olson/Shutterstock Images, 18; © Alex Staroseltsev/Shutterstock Images, 20

Library of Congress Cataloging-in-Publication Data
Names: Labrecque, Ellen, author.
Title: Ada Lovelace and computer algorithms / by Ellen Labrecque.
Description: Ann Arbor : Cherry Lake Publishing, [2017] | Series: Women innovators | Audience: K to grade 3. | Includes bibliographical references and index.
Identifiers: LCCN 2016029695| ISBN 9781634721776 (hardcover) | ISBN 9781634722438 (pdf) | ISBN 9781634723091 (pbk.) | ISBN 9781634723756 (ebook)
Subjects: LCSH: Lovelace, Ada King, Countess of, 1815-1852–Juvenile literature. | Women mathematicians–Great Britain–Biography–Juvenile literature. | Women computer programmers–Great Britain–Biography–Juvenile literature. | Mathematicians–Great Britain–Biography–Juvenile literature. | Computer programmers–Great Britain–Biography–Juvenile literature. | Computers–History–19th century–Juvenile literature. | Computer algorithms–History–19th century–Juvenile literature.
Classification: LCC QA29.L72 L33 2017 | DDC 510.92 [B]–dc23
LC record available at https://lccn.loc.gov/2016029695

Cherry Lake Publishing would like to acknowledge the work of The Partnership for 21st Century Skills. Please visit *www.p21.org* for more information.

Printed in the United States of America
Corporate Graphics

CONTENTS

Computers are an important part of everyday life.

A Woman

Do you use a computer? Maybe you use it to do your homework. Or maybe you play video games on it. Thanks to the people who created them, computers do many different things.

Ada Lovelace was the world's first **computer programmer**. She was born more than 200 years ago. Without her, computers would not be what they are today!

Lovelace's independence and interest in math made her an unusual woman for her time.

Augusta Ada Lovelace was born on December 10, 1815, in London, England. Her dad was the famous poet Lord Byron. Her mom was Annabella Byron. Her parents separated soon after Ada was born. Her mom raised her.

For centuries, people tried and failed to create a successful flying machine.

Ada's mom wanted her to study hard. She hired tutors to teach her daughter every subject. Ada was good in math and science. And like her poet father, she saw beauty in everything. Ada loved machines. She wanted to build a flying one someday.

Create!

Ada designed a flying machine long before airplanes ever existed. Can you create a new machine? Make a detailed drawing of your new **invention**. Include instructions about how it will work.

Charles Babbage thought math could be done more easily with a machine.

When Ada was 17, she met the famous **mathematician** Charles Babbage. The two became friends. Babbage created a machine called the Analytical Engine. It was one of the first computers that could solve complex math problems.

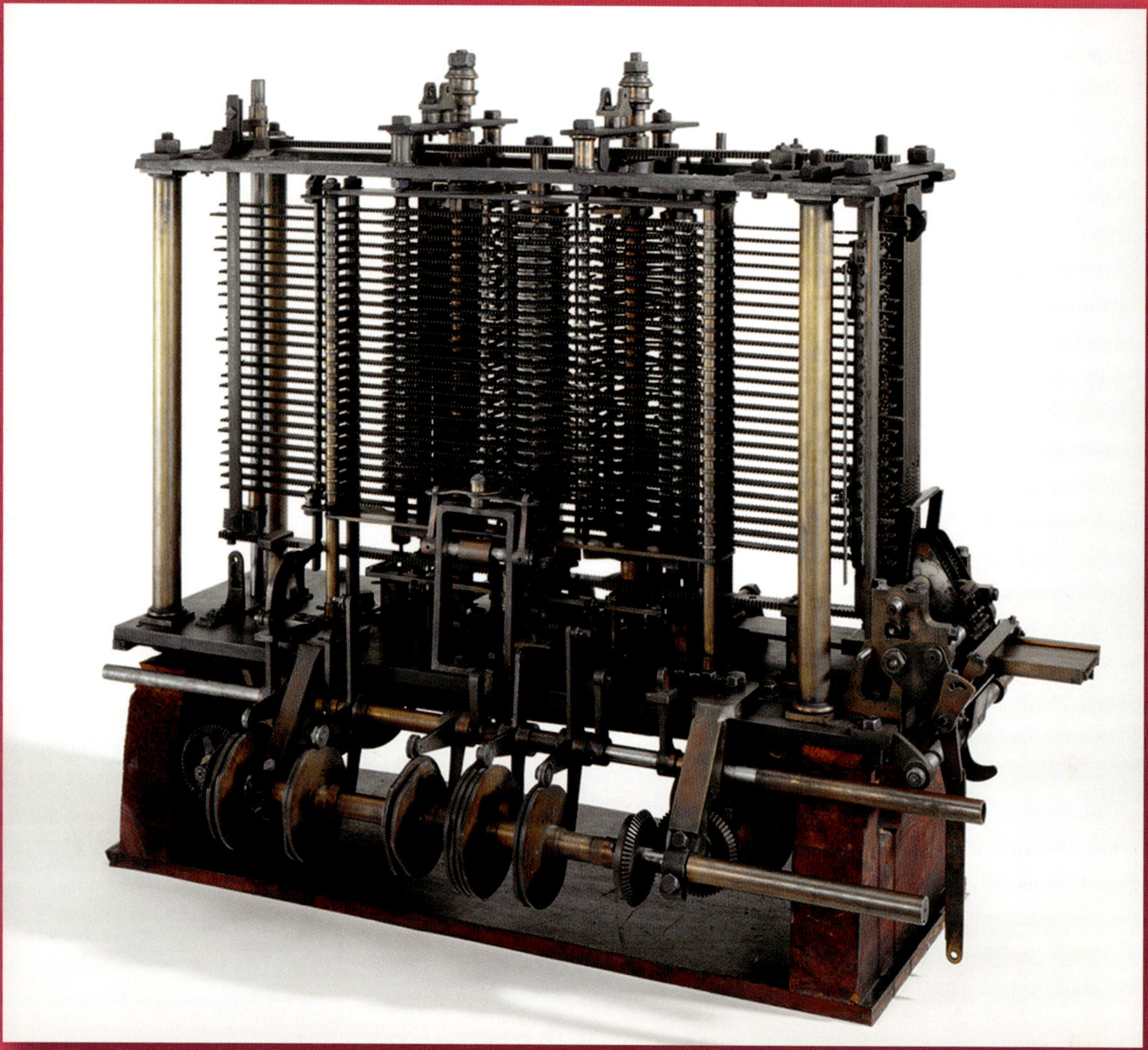

Today, you can see the Analytical Engine at the Science Museum in London.

An Idea

Babbage taught Lovelace many things about math. She soon began working with him. She helped him by writing an **algorithm** for the Analytical Engine.

Look!

Look at this photo of the Analytical Engine. Do you think computers today are easier or harder to use? Why?

Diagram for the computation by the Engine of the Numbers of Bernoulli. See Note G. (page 722 *et seq.*)

Number of Operation.	Nature of Operation.	Variables acted upon.	Variables receiving results.	Indication of change in the value on any Variable.	Statement of Results.	Data.			Working Variables.									
						${}^1V_1$ ○ 0 0 0 1 [1]	${}^1V_2$ ○ 0 0 0 2 [2]	${}^1V_3$ ○ 0 0 0 4 [n]	${}^0V_4$ ○ 0 0 0 0	${}^0V_5$ ○ 0 0 0 0	${}^0V_6$ ○ 0 0 0 0	${}^0V_7$ ○ 0 0 0 0	${}^0V_8$ ○ 0 0 0 0	${}^0V_9$ ○ 0 0 0 0	${}^0V_{10}$ ○ 0 0 0 0	${}^0V_{11}$ ○ 0 0 0 0	${}^0V_{12}$ ○ 0 0 0 0	
1	×	${}^1V_2 \times {}^1V_3$	${}^1V_4, {}^1V_5, {}^1V_6$	$\left\{\begin{matrix}{}^1V_2={}^1V_2\\{}^1V_3={}^1V_3\end{matrix}\right\}$	$=2n$	...	2	n	$2n$	$2n$	$2n$							
2	−	${}^1V_4 - {}^1V_1$	${}^2V_4$	$\left\{\begin{matrix}{}^1V_4={}^2V_4\\{}^1V_1={}^1V_1\end{matrix}\right\}$	$=2n-1$	1	...	...	$2n-1$									
3	+	${}^1V_5 + {}^1V_1$	${}^2V_5$	$\left\{\begin{matrix}{}^1V_5={}^2V_5\\{}^1V_1={}^1V_1\end{matrix}\right\}$	$=2n+1$	1	...	...	...	$2n+1$								
4	÷	${}^2V_5 \div {}^2V_4$	${}^1V_{11}$	$\left\{\begin{matrix}{}^2V_5={}^0V_5\\{}^2V_4={}^0V_4\end{matrix}\right\}$	$=\frac{2n-1}{2n+1}$	...	...	...	0	0	...	...	...	...	...	$\frac{2n-1}{2n+1}$		
5	÷	${}^1V_{11} \div {}^1V_2$	${}^2V_{11}$	$\left\{\begin{matrix}{}^1V_{11}={}^2V_{11}\\{}^1V_2={}^1V_2\end{matrix}\right\}$	$=\frac{1}{2}\cdot\frac{2n-1}{2n+1}$	...	2	...	...	...	...	...	...	...	...	$\frac{1}{2}\cdot\frac{2n-1}{2n+1}$		
6	−	${}^0V_{13} - {}^2V_{11}$	${}^1V_{13}$	$\left\{\begin{matrix}{}^2V_{11}={}^0V_{11}\\{}^0V_{13}={}^1V_{13}\end{matrix}\right\}$	$=-\frac{1}{2}\cdot\frac{2n-1}{2n+1}=A_0$	...	...	...	...	...	...	...	...	...	...	0	....	$-\frac{1}{2}$
7	−	${}^1V_3 - {}^1V_1$	${}^1V_{10}$	$\left\{\begin{matrix}{}^1V_3={}^1V_3\\{}^1V_1={}^1V_1\end{matrix}\right\}$	$=n-1\ (=3)$	1	...	n	...	...	...	...	...	...	$n-1$			
8	+	${}^1V_2 + {}^0V_7$	${}^1V_7$	$\left\{\begin{matrix}{}^1V_2={}^1V_2\\{}^0V_7={}^1V_7\end{matrix}\right\}$	$=2+0=2$	...	2	...	...	...	...	2						
9	÷	${}^1V_6 \div {}^1V_7$	${}^3V_{11}$	$\left\{\begin{matrix}{}^1V_6={}^1V_6\\{}^0V_{11}={}^3V_{11}\end{matrix}\right\}$	$=\frac{2n}{2}=A_1$	...	...	...	...	...	$2n$	2	...	...	...	$\frac{2n}{2}=A_1$		
10	×	${}^1V_{21} \times {}^3V_{11}$	${}^1V_{12}$	$\left\{\begin{matrix}{}^1V_{21}={}^1V_{21}\\{}^3V_{11}={}^3V_{11}\end{matrix}\right\}$	$=B_1\cdot\frac{2n}{2}=B_1A_1$	...	...	...	...	...	...	...	...	...	...	$\frac{2n}{2}=A_1$	$B_1\cdot\frac{2n}{2}=B_1A_1$	
11	+	${}^1V_{12} + {}^1V_{13}$	${}^2V_{13}$	$\left\{\begin{matrix}{}^1V_{12}={}^0V_{12}\\{}^1V_{13}={}^2V_{13}\end{matrix}\right\}$	$=-\frac{1}{2}\cdot\frac{2n-1}{2n+1}+B_1\cdot\frac{2n}{2}$	...	...	...	...	...	...	...	...	...	...	....	0	$\left\{-\frac{1}{2}\cdot\right.$
12	−	${}^1V_{10} - {}^1V_1$	${}^2V_{10}$	$\left\{\begin{matrix}{}^1V_{10}={}^2V_{10}\\{}^1V_1={}^1V_1\end{matrix}\right\}$	$=n-2\ (=2)$	1	...	...	...	...	...	...	...	...	$n-2$			
13	−	${}^1V_6 - {}^1V_1$	${}^2V_6$	$\left\{\begin{matrix}{}^1V_6={}^2V_6\\{}^1V_1={}^1V_1\end{matrix}\right\}$	$=2n-1$	1	...	...	...	...	$2n-1$							
14	+	${}^1V_1 + {}^1V_7$	${}^2V_7$	$\left\{\begin{matrix}{}^1V_1={}^1V_1\\{}^1V_7={}^2V_7\end{matrix}\right\}$	$=2+1=3$	1	...	...	...	...	...	3						
15	÷	${}^2V_6 \div {}^2V_7$	${}^1V_8$	$\left\{\begin{matrix}{}^2V_6={}^2V_6\\{}^2V_7={}^2V_7\end{matrix}\right\}$	$=\frac{2n-1}{3}$	...	...	...	...	...	$2n-1$	3	$\frac{2n-1}{3}$					
16	×	${}^1V_8 \times {}^3V_{11}$	${}^4V_{11}$	$\left\{\begin{matrix}{}^1V_8={}^0V_8\\{}^3V_{11}={}^4V_{11}\end{matrix}\right\}$	$=\frac{2n}{2}\cdot\frac{2n-1}{3}$	...	...	...	...	...	...	...	0	...	...	$\frac{2n}{2}\cdot\frac{2n-1}{3}$		
17	−	${}^2V_6 - {}^1V_1$	${}^3V_6$	$\left\{\begin{matrix}{}^2V_6={}^3V_6\\{}^1V_1={}^1V_1\end{matrix}\right\}$	$=2n-2$	1	...	...	...	...	$2n-2$							
18	+	${}^1V_1 + {}^2V_7$	${}^3V_7$	$\left\{\begin{matrix}{}^2V_7={}^3V_7\\{}^1V_1={}^1V_1\end{matrix}\right\}$	$=3+1=4$	1	...	...	...	...	...	4						
19	÷	${}^3V_6 \div {}^3V_7$	${}^1V_9$	$\left\{\begin{matrix}{}^3V_6={}^3V_6\\{}^3V_7={}^3V_7\end{matrix}\right\}$	$=\frac{2n-2}{4}$	...	...	...	...	...	$2n-2$	4	...	$\frac{2n-2}{4}$	...	$\left\{\frac{2n}{2}\cdot\frac{2n-1}{3}\cdot\frac{2n-2}{3}=A_3\right\}$		
20	×	${}^1V_9 \times {}^4V_{11}$	${}^5V_{11}$	$\left\{\begin{matrix}{}^1V_9={}^0V_9\\{}^4V_{11}={}^5V_{11}\end{matrix}\right\}$	$=\frac{2n}{2}\cdot\frac{2n-1}{3}\cdot\frac{2n-2}{4}=A_3$	...	...	...	...	...	...	...	...	0				
21	×	${}^1V_{22} \times {}^5V_{11}$	${}^0V_{12}$	$\left\{\begin{matrix}{}^1V_{22}={}^1V_{22}\\{}^0V_{12}={}^2V_{12}\end{matrix}\right\}$	$=B_3\cdot\frac{2n}{2}\cdot\frac{2n-1}{3}\cdot\frac{2n-2}{3}=B_3A_3$	...	...	...	...	...	...	...	...	...	...	0	B_3A_3	
22	+	${}^2V_{12} + {}^2V_{13}$	${}^3V_{13}$	$\left\{\begin{matrix}{}^2V_{12}={}^0V_{12}\\{}^2V_{13}={}^3V_{13}\end{matrix}\right\}$	$=A_0+B_1A_1+B_3A_3$	...	...	...	...	...	...	...	...	...	...	....	0	$\left\{A_3+\right.$
23	−	${}^2V_{10} - {}^1V_1$	${}^3V_{10}$	$\left\{\begin{matrix}{}^2V_{10}={}^3V_{10}\\{}^1V_1={}^1V_1\end{matrix}\right\}$	$=n-3\ (=1)$	1	...	...	...	...	...	...	...	...	$n-3$			
					Here follows a repetition of Operations thirteen to twenty-three.													
24	+	${}^4V_{13} + {}^0V_{24}$	${}^1V_{24}$	$\left\{\begin{matrix}{}^4V_{13}={}^0V_{13}\\{}^0V_{24}={}^1V_{24}\end{matrix}\right\}$	$=B_7$	...	...	...	...	...	...	...	...	...	...	....	....	
25	+	${}^1V_1 + {}^1V_3$	${}^1V_3$	$\left\{\begin{matrix}{}^1V_1={}^1V_1\\{}^1V_3={}^1V_3\\{}^5V_6={}^0V_6\\{}^5V_7={}^0V_7\end{matrix}\right\}$	$=n+1=4+1=5$ by a Variable-card. by a Variable card.	1	...	$n+1$	...	...	0	0						

This is the code that Lovelace wrote for the Analytical Engine.

Lovelace used a series of numbers for her algorithm. She also wrote notes about the machine for Babbage. Her notes explained how the machine could learn to repeat a series of instructions over and over. This is called **looping**, and it is still used today. Lovelace's algorithm and notes are considered to be the world's first computer program!

Think!

Where are algorithms used in everyday life? Can you use an algorithm to make a grilled cheese sandwich? Could you use an algorithm to solve a Rubik's Cube? Think of other places where algorithms are found.

Computers help musicians record, improve, and share their music.

A Legacy

Lovelace died of cancer at age 36. But her **legacy** of ideas helped shape the computers we know today. Lovelace was one of the first people to think machines could be used for more than numbers. She thought they could even be programmed to make music. She was right!

Today, coding isn't just for adults. Kids can learn to code their own games and Web sites.

In 1979, the United States Department of Defense came up with a new computer language. The language was named Ada, in honor of Lovelace. Ada is still used in computer **software** today!

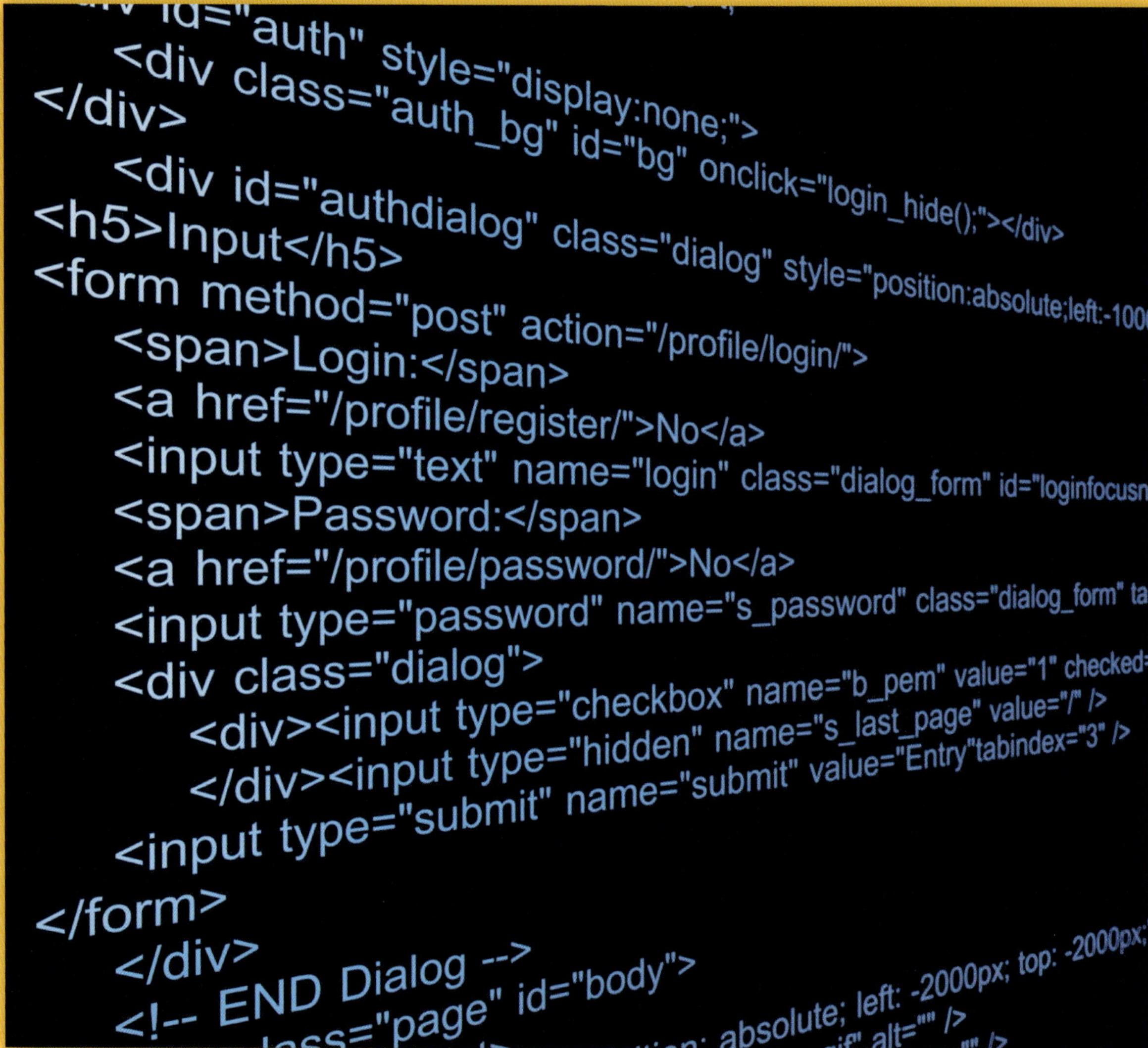

This computer code is called HTML. It is used to make Web sites.

We live in the **digital age**. Computers play a big part in our everyday lives. We use them in almost everything we do. All computers use special languages to help them run. These languages are made up of numbers, symbols, and letters. Ada Lovelace was one of the first inventors to help create these languages. She was also the first person to understand how powerful machines could be. Without Lovelace, the world would be much different than it is today!

GLOSSARY

algorithm (AL-guh-rith-uhm) a set of step-by-step instructions for solving a problem

computer programmer (kuhm-PYOO-tur PROH-gram-ur) a person who writes the instructions to make a computer run

digital age (DIJ-ih-tuhl AYJ) the time period we live in where most people have computers and smartphones, which help people easily get and share information

invention (in-VEN-shun) something new created from imagination

legacy (LEG-uh-see) something handed down from one generation to another

looping (LOO-ping) an order of instructions for a computer that are repeated over and over until the task is completed

mathematician (math-uh-muh-TISH-uhn) an expert in the study of math

software (SAWFT-wair) the programs used to make a computer work

FIND OUT MORE

BOOKS

Stanley, Diane. *Ada Lovelace, Poet of Science: The First Computer Programmer*. New York: Simon and Schuster, 2016.

Thimmesh, Catherine. *Girls Think of Everything: Stories of Ingenious Inventions by Women*. New York: HMH Books for Young Readers, 2002.

Wallmark, Laurie. *Ada Byron Lovelace and the Thinking Machine*. Berkeley, CA: Creston Books, 2015.

WEB SITES

Computer History Museum—The Babbage Engine

www.computerhistory.org/babbage/adalovelace
Learn more about Ada Lovelace and the history of computers.

Scratch

https://scratch.mit.edu
Learn how to do your own coding and computer programming.

INDEX

ABOUT THE AUTHOR

Ellen Labrecque is a freelance writer living in Yardley, Pennsylvania. Previously, she was a senior editor at Sports Illustrated Kids. Ellen loves to travel and then learn about new places and people that she can write about in her books.